MANALI CHRONICLES

THE TRIP

BUDHA DEV MUKHERJEE

Made with ❤ on the Notion Press Platform
www.notionpress.com

Dedicated to me, the movies i cherish and the articles i get to read on Internet.

Contents

CHAPTER I

The Nightmare

Aarav awoke with a start, sweat pouring down his face. His heart was pounding in his chest. "Are you okay?" asked Raghav, handing him a water bottle.

"I think so," Aarav replied, taking a sip of water to calm himself. "I just had that nightmare again. The same man and woman, but I still can't see their faces."

Raghav sighed sympathetically. "I know you have this dream a lot, but try not to think about it. Tomorrow is our final exam, and after that, we finally get to go on our trip to Manali."

Aarav nodded, feeling a rush of excitement at the thought of their upcoming adventure. "Yeah, you're right. I'll try to get some rest. Thanks, Raghav."

Raghav smiled and patted his shoulder. "No problem, man. We've got this." And with that, the two friends settled back into their beds and drifted off to sleep, ready to tackle the day ahead.

"Wake up, everyone!" Shivam called out, "We've got an exam today and need to be fully alert." Raghav groaned, "Just a moment, man. Aarav woke us up with his screaming again last night."

"That's just par for the course," Shivam added with a smile, "He's been doing this since the day we started sharing this place. The guy just can't seem to shake the creepy vibes from all those horror novels he devours every day."

"Come on guys!" Shivam encouraged, giving Aarav a gentle shake, "Time to wake up. We don't want to be late for our exam." Aarav and Raghav quickly jumped out of bed and the three of them raced to the examination centre, eager to make the most of the day ahead.

CHAPTER II

Daydreaming about Manali

"Time is valuable, gentlemen," the invigilator stated firmly as the three of them entered the classroom, a few minutes late for the exam. They took their seats with heads bowed, ready to focus on the task at hand and make the most of their remaining time.

Aarav found his mind wandering to the stunning vistas of Manali, while his classmates were grappling with the questions on the exam paper. Suddenly, Ankita jolted him back to reality with a gentle tap on the arm, "Hey, stay focused on the task at hand." With a nod of agreement, Aarav refocused his attention on the exam, determined to give it his all.

Aarav shot Ankita a look of disapproval, then refocused on finishing his exam.

Just then, the invigilator called out, "Time's up, students!" He began collecting the papers and addressed the class with a touch of irony, "I trust you all wrote enough answers to secure a passing grade." Aarav muttered something under his breath, barely audible.

As the students began to exit the classroom, Ankita turned to Aarav with a scolding tone, "What were you thinking during the exam, daydreaming like that?"

Aarav chuckled, "I was lost in the beauty of the majestic mountain ranges."

Shivam chimed in, "Let it go, Ankita. Aarav here lives in his own little world of fantasy. Speaking of which, we're headed to Manali tomorrow, care to join us?"

Ankita sighed, "Unfortunately, I can’t make it. I have my cousin’s engagement ceremony tomorrow."

"Come on guys, let’s get our bags packed for tomorrow!" Raghav cried out with excitement. "Take care, Ankita! We’ll see you soon."

Ankita waved goodbye, "Have a blast, guys!"

CHAPTER III

Arrived in Manali

"Time is valuable, gentlemen," the invigilator stated firmly as the three of them entered the classroom, a few minutes late for the exam. They took their seats with heads bowed, ready to focus on the task at hand and make the most of their remaining time.

Aarav found his mind wandering to the stunning vistas of Manali, while his classmates were grappling with the questions on the exam paper. Suddenly, Ankita jolted him back to reality with a gentle tap on the arm, "Hey, stay focused on the task at hand." With a nod of agreement, Aarav refocused his attention on the exam, determined to give it his all.

Aarav shot Ankita a look of disapproval, then refocused on finishing his exam.

Just then, the invigilator called out, "Time's up, students!" He began collecting the papers and addressed the class with a touch of irony, "I trust you all wrote enough answers to secure a passing grade." Aarav muttered something under his breath, barely audible.

As the students began to exit the classroom, Ankita turned to Aarav with a scolding tone, "What were you thinking during the exam, daydreaming like that?"

Aarav chuckled, "I was lost in the beauty of the majestic mountain ranges."

Shivam chimed in, "Let it go, Ankita. Aarav here lives in his own little world of fantasy. Speaking of which, we're headed to Manali tomorrow, care to join us?"

Ankita sighed, "Unfortunately, I can't make it. I have my cousin's engagement ceremony tomorrow."

"Come on guys, let's get our bags packed for tomorrow!" Raghav cried out with excitement. "Take care, Ankita! We'll see you soon."

Ankita waved goodbye, "Have a blast, guys!"

……

The next day, the excitement kept them up all night.

"It's time to go!" Shivam announced, "The taxi is waiting for us outside." The trio headed to the airport, eager to embark on the adventure of a lifetime and make memories that would last a lifetime.

After a three-hour journey, they finally arrived at Manali, the picturesque valley known as the abode of gods. They took a taxi to their homestay, and as they journeyed through the breathtaking landscape, it was as if they were transported into a page from Ruskin Bond's novel. Aarav initiated a chat with the taxi driver, and soon enough, Raghav and Shivam joined in. They discussed all the must-visit tourist spots, cultural experiences to immerse in, and delectable dishes to try during their stay in Manali.

They reached their homestay after a brief 15-minute drive and were greeted by a massive structure that looked like a cluster of bamboo cottages. They walked through the tiny gate and rapped on the vibrant blue door. A cheerful young woman greeted them with a warm smile as she opened the door. "Ah, you must be from Kolkata!" she exclaimed. Raghav stepped forward and confirmed, "Yes, ma'am. We have booked a three-day stay here."

"Please come in and make yourselves comfortable," the young lady invited. "I'll just call my husband, and he'll take care of the formalities." The trio took a seat in the cosy waiting area and left their luggage in the entrance hall. The reception was adorned with intricate bamboo handicrafts, a key holder displaying a variety of keys, charming wall paintings, and a magnificent jhoomar hanging from the ceiling.

A young man's voice boomed from behind, "Welcome to Manali, folks!" He introduced himself and his wife, "I'm Raju, and this is my wife Kanika. We'll be your hosts during your stay." After completing the necessary paperwork, Raju retrieved the key from the key holder and motioned for the three of them to follow him.

When Raju led them to their room, they were awestruck by its beauty. It was a spacious room with magnificent Kullu valley wall paintings, ample windows, and a stunning balcony that offered panoramic views of the mountains.

"Make yourselves at home and freshen up. I'll be back shortly with breakfast," Raju said as he left the room. Aarav rushed to the balcony, entranced by the vista before him. "We have to climb that mountain after breakfast!" he exclaimed, his eyes shining with excitement. While Raghav set up his 'Manali' playlist, Shivam began capturing the scenery with his camera.

Before long, Raju returned with a tray overflowing with delectable breakfast items: bread, omelettes, cheese, and freshly squeezed orange juice. The scrumptious meal, paired with the breathtaking view, was more than they could have ever hoped for. They snapped a few photos to post on Instagram before digging in and savouring every bite. Once they finished, they were eager to venture out and explore the surroundings.

Raghav issued a challenge to his friends, "Let's see who can reach the mountains first!" "Challenge accepted," replied Aarav and Shivam, eager for a competition.

CHAPTER IV

The Dark Turn

They set off at a sprint, but soon realised they were overexerting themselves and needed a break.

"Let's head over to that gorgeous river and rest for a bit," Aarav suggested, pointing in its direction. They made their way to the riverbank and found a large boulder to sit on. They marvelled at the stunning valley before them, with a verdant forest at its base and a shimmering river meandering through it.

"Time flies when you're surrounded by beauty," Shivam said as he realised they had been admiring the mountains for three hours. "It's time to head back and refuel with a hearty meal."

As they walked back to their lodging, Raghav suggested an exciting detour. "How about we explore that lush jungle over there?" he pointed to a nearby forest.

Excited by the idea, Shivam exclaimed, "Let's do it! A walk through the jungle sounds like a perfect adventure."

With eager steps, they set off to discover the wonders of the jungle and create new memories.

Aarav stepped into the lush jungle, admiring its beauty. "This place is breathtaking! Can you take a picture of me here?" he asked Raghav.

"Sure thing," Raghav replied, reaching for his camera.

But before he could snap the shot, a strange noise echoed through the jungle. Raghav's ears perked up. "Guys, did you hear that? Something's not right," he said, turning to his friends.

Aarav's eyes grew wide with fear. "Yes, I heard it too. I think there are wild animals in this jungle," he said, his voice shaking.

Just then, they heard a clear and desperate feminine voice calling out from deeper in the jungle. "Please help us!"

The three friends looked at each other, realising they needed to act quickly. They quickly gathered their things and made their way back to the safety of the trailhead.

"Quick, let's head inside. I think a woman is in need of assistance," Shivam urged, leading the way. As they made their way through the narrow, muddied path, the cries grew louder and more urgent. When they finally reached the source of the commotion, they were met with a shocking sight. A man was gasping for air and a woman lay on the ground, her clothes soaked with blood and her cries for help echoing through the area. Shivam and his companion sprang into action, determined to do all they could to help those in need.

Shivam approached the injured woman, his heart sinking as he recognized her as Kanika and the man next to her as Raju, their generous hosts. Aarav quickly sprang into action, searching for a means of transportation to take them to the hospital. Raghav, meanwhile, attempted to call for emergency assistance, but his efforts were in vain as he was met with no response.

Recognizing the urgency of the situation, Raghav suggested they seek help from the nearby community. The trio quickly spotted a small bamboo cottage and approached it, determined to find the help they needed for Kanika and Raju.

CHAPTER V

The Old Man

They hurried up to the cottage and urgently knocked on the door, which was answered by an elderly man in his late 80s. "Please, sir, there's a couple who are injured in the jungle," Aarav implored. "We need your help to save them."

After a moment of consideration, the elderly man invited them inside and offered them tea. Aarav and his friends were taken aback by the man's composed demeanour, especially given the urgency of the situation. "Sir, we must act quickly to save them," Aarav emphasised.

Shivam and the others entered the old man's home, unsure of what to expect. The man greeted them warmly, inviting them in and assuring them that he would help. The single room was modest, with a mattress in the corner and a table filled with medicine and a tray of tea. Sunlight streamed in through a leak in the ceiling. Despite their puzzlement and tension, the old man offered them tea, which they politely declined.

"Kanika was my daughter," the old man said, his gaze distant.

Shivam and the others spoke up in unison. "But sir, she's still alive. We can save her and her husband is there too."

The old man's eyes lit up with hope. "Then let's not waste any time," he said, determined in his voice. "We'll do everything in our power to bring her back home safely."

Aarav, Raghav, and Shivam listened in shock as the old man recounted the events of two years prior. "Kanika and Raju were murdered by four men," he said, his voice cracking with emotion. "It happened on a December afternoon, when I was away at a relative's wedding. Kanika was staying at my cottage, while Raju was in the jungle picking berries. When he encountered a group of tourists who were drinking and littering, he approached them and asked them to respect the area and stop drinking. But instead of listening, the tourists began to abuse and push him. Raju always carried a pocket knife for protection, and he pulled it out to threaten the men. They were scared and apologised, but it was too late." The old man finished his story, tears streaming down his face, as the three young men sat in stunned silence.

The old man's story took a darker turn as he continued. "One of the tourists snuck up behind Raju and strangled him with a rope. Despite Raju's struggles and cries for help, he couldn't escape his attacker," the old man said, his voice trembling with grief. "Kanika went into the forest to find her husband, calling out his name. But when she saw his lifeless body surrounded by the four men, she knew what had happened. Overcome with rage and sorrow, she took Raju's pocket knife and approached the attackers. But before she could act, one of them grabbed her from behind and pushed her to the ground. In a final act of defiance, she used the knife to end her own life before they could harm her." The old man finished his tale, tears still streaming down his face. "All of the perpetrators fled and were never caught by the authorities," he said, his voice heavy with regret.

Raghav shuddered with fear as the old man finished his story, while Shivam gazed intently into the old man's eyes. Aarav, however, was still confused. "Sir, we checked into their house and had breakfast prepared for us by them. How can they be dead?" he asked, trying to reconcile the story with his own experience.

The old man's tears flowed freely as he spoke. "They've come back as ghosts to seek vengeance by tricking tourists and killing them. You're lucky to have come to me," he said, his voice trembling with emotion. "Now go, save yourselves."

CHAPTER VI

The Escape

Aarav, Raghav, and Shivam looked at each other in terror, realising the truth of what they had encountered. They stood up, unable to find the words to console the old man for his loss, but grateful to have escaped the ghostly trap. They thanked him and quickly left, their minds racing with fear and confusion.

As the three of them started to run, Aarav's phone slipped from his pocket and went unnoticed. The sun had already set, casting the sky in darkness, and the moonlight shone eerily around them as they raced down the deserted road. Suddenly, they noticed headlights behind them and turned to see a bus approaching.

The three of them boarded the bus and found seats in a quiet corner, too scared to even make eye contact with each other. As the bus pulled over to a stop, a group of ladies boarded and politely asked them to move as they were sitting in the designated seating area for women. The three friends were jolted back to reality by the conductor's shout, and they quickly stood up. Aarav spoke up, "My aunt lives in Chandigarh. We can take a bus there. It should take us about 6 to 7 hours." Raghav and Shivam nodded in agreement, and the three of them set off on their journey, still shaken by the events of the evening.

As the conductor approached their seats, the three friends asked him to stop the bus at the next stand. Aarav remembered that he needed to call his aunt and let her know they were on their way. "I should contact my aunt to inquire about her current address, as I visited her when I was 13 years old. She'll send my cousin to pick us up from the bus station," he said, reaching into his pocket. But then his face fell, "Oh no! I must have dropped my phone near the old man's house."

As the bus pulled to a stop, the conductor announced that their stop had arrived. The three friends quickly gathered their belongings and stepped down from the bus. They were immediately approached by several cab drivers offering their services.

"We have to go back and retrieve Aarav's phone. We need it to contact his aunt," Shivam said.

Raghav nodded, "Yeah, let's take a cab."

CHAPTER VII

Reality or Fiction?

Aarav stepped forward and negotiated with one of the drivers, and soon they were on their way back down the eerie road. The once peaceful and serene countryside now felt like it was straight out of a horror novel. The silence was only broken by the sound of the wheels against the gravel road, and the boys felt their nerves build with every passing mile. Suddenly, the driver brought the car to a halt and announced, "It looks like there's been an accident ahead. I'll be back in a bit." Aarav peered outside and recognized the surroundings immediately. This was the same place where Kanika and Raju had sought help from them. Without hesitation, Aarav stepped out of the vehicle, eager to see what was causing the commotion.

As Aarav approached the police barricade, he saw a crowd of onlookers gathered around. He made his way to the nearest officer and asked, "Excuse me, officer. What happened here?" Aarav's heart sank as the officer spoke. He felt a chill run down his spine, and he felt a wave of fear and disbelief wash over him. He stepped back from the officer and walked back to the car, his mind racing. "What did he say?" Raghav and Shivam asked in unison as he got back into the car.

"The couple we saw was murdered," Aarav said, his voice barely audible. "And the officer said that it's the fifth murder in a week, all found in the same location." The three friends sat in stunned silence as the reality of what they had just learned settled in. They decided to leave the area as soon as possible and get to Aarav's aunt's place in

Chandigarh, where they could seek safety and gather their thoughts.

Aarav's thoughts raced as he realised the old man's story was full of inconsistencies and holes. "Could it be possible that the old man was actually one of the killers?" Aarav thought to himself, his mind reeling with the possibility. While narrating the story, the old man stated that no one was present when his daughter was murdered, and that he, too, was out of town at the time, so how did he know the killers were four men who were tourists? Because they were never arrested. How did he narrate the story in such detail if he was not present at the incident? He had three extra cups of tea on the table, how did that happen?

With a sense of urgency, Aarav stepped out of the car and broke into a run. His heart was pounding with a mix of fear and determination.The desire to clarify things overpowered Aarav's fear, and he began running towards the old man's house.

As Aarav picked up speed, he suddenly stumbled, his foot catching on something unseen. He stumbled forward, barely managing to regain his balance. He glanced down, confused. The road was clear and empty, with no rocks or obstacles in sight. What had caused him to trip?

CHAPTER VIII

The Final Chapter

He stood up and found himself transported to a different reality. He was standing in front of the old man's house, but it looked different. The house was made of stones, and the door was made of iron. He pushed the door, and it creaked open, revealing a dark and eerie interior. Aarav hesitated for a moment, but his determination to find answers pushed him forward.

He entered the house and called out for the old man, but there was no response. Aarav felt a shiver run down his spine as he walked deeper into the house. The walls were adorned with eerie paintings and the floorboards creaked under his feet. Suddenly, he heard a noise coming from the room at the end of the hall. He cautiously approached the room and pushed the door open.

To his surprise, the old man was sitting in front of a fireplace, staring into the fire. Aarav approached him and asked, "Why did you lie to us? Why did you deceive us?" The old man slowly turned his head and looked at Aarav with piercing eyes. "You need to understand, son. The past is always better left buried. Sometimes, the truth is too cruel to face."

Aarav's heart sank and as he approached the old man, he stumbled back and found himself back on the deserted road, his body shaking, and his mind reeling.

Suddenly, a beam of intense light approached him, growing brighter with each passing moment. Aarav shielded his eyes, squinting against the glare as he tried to make out the source of the light. He was trying to adjust to the sudden brightness, and when he finally opened his eyes, he was shocked by what he saw. As the light faded, the outlines of a man and a woman gradually came into view, their faces becoming clearer with each passing moment. Aarav rubbed his eyes, unsure if what he was seeing was real.

As the shadows took shape, Kanika and Raju emerged, their faces now fully visible.

To be continued...

9 798889 595168

Printed by Libri Plureos GmbH in Hamburg,
Germany